After School Club

Starring Sammie . . .

. . . as the girl who becomes a big fat liar
(but whose pants *don't* catch fire)

Helena Pielichaty
Illustrated by Melanie Williamson

OXFORD
UNIVERSITY PRESS

OXFORD
UNIVERSITY PRESS

Great Clarendon Street, Oxford OX2 6DP

Oxford University Press is a department of the University of Oxford.
It furthers the University's objective of excellence in research, scholarship,
and education by publishing worldwide in

Oxford New York

Auckland Bangkok Buenos Aires Cape Town
Chennai Dar es Salaam Delhi Hong Kong Istanbul Karachi
Kolkata Kuala Lumpur Madrid Melbourne Mexico City Mumbai
Nairobi São Paulo Shanghai Taipei Tokyo Toronto

Oxford is a registered trade mark of Oxford University Press
in the UK and in certain other countries

Copyright © Helena Pielichaty 2003

The moral rights of the author have been asserted

Database right Oxford University Press (maker)

First published 2003

British Library Cataloguing in Publication Data available

ISBN 0-19-275247-2

1 3 5 7 9 10 8 6 4 2

Designed and typeset by Mike Brain Graphic Design Limited, Oxford

Printed in Great Britain by Cox & Wyman Ltd, Reading, Berkshire

to Connor James Fitzgerald,
a little diamond geezer
with love

Welcome to
ZAPS

Contact: Jan Fryston NNEB (Supervisor)
on 07734-090876 for details.

Please note: Mr Sharkey, headmaster of Zetland Avenue
Primary School, politely requests parents/carers <u>not</u> to
contact the school directly as the After School Club is
independent of the school and he wants it to stay that way!

All children must be registered before they attend.

Zetland Avenue Primary School (ZAPS) After School Club

Newsletter

Dear Parents and Carers,

We have lots of exciting things planned for this year and hope you will tell your friends and neighbours all about us. Children do not have to attend Zetland Avenue Primary School to come to After School Club; any child is welcome as long as they are aged between five and eleven and have been registered.

Special Events:

1. November: **Children in Need Fundraising.** We will be joining in with the main school's activities. We wonder what Mr Sharkey will be getting up to this year? (If you remember, last year he sat in a bath of smelly jelly!)

2. February half-term holiday: **Film-making Week.** Media Studies students from Bretton Hill College will be showing us how to make and star in a real film. Watch out, Hollywood!

3. Easter: **Pop Kids.** We will be staging a talent show to perform in front of parents and carers.

4. Summer: **Get Active!** Summer Sports activities for everyone throughout the holidays.

Also: E-PALS

Once the new computers have been installed we are hoping to set up an Internet connection to After School Clubs throughout the UK. Children who are interested will be able to write to their 'E-pals' from Penzance to Pitlochry!

See you all soon,

Jan

Jan Fryston (Supervisor)

After School Club

Sammie Wesley

Reggie Glazzard

Alex McCormack

Lloyd Fountain

Mrs Fryston
Supervisor

Mrs McCormack
Assistant

Brody Miller

Sam Riley

Jolene Nevin

Brandon Petty

Some comments from our customers at the After School Club:

'It's better than going round my gran's and having to watch Kung Fu films all day in the holidays'—

Brandon Petty, Y1

'It's good because I am home-schooled so the After School Club gives me a chance to mix with children my own age and make new friends.'

Lloyd Fountain, aged 9

'I love going to ZAPS After School Club— there's so much to do. It's a blast.'

(Brody Miller, Y6)

— You feel at ease
— On the purple settees
— The staff are kind
— And help you unwind
— So come along
— You can't go wrong

— (Sam Riley, Y5)

'After School Club is OK, apart from the rats and poisonous biscuits.' (Don't worry folks – just messing with your minds – Ha! Ha!)

Reggie G. aged 133*

*our resident comedian informs me he prefers to use months to describe his age – JF

'There's not nowhere better than After School Club and I like Mrs Fryston because she is kind and understands how you feel about things.'

Sammie Wesley Y5

'I've been to other After School Clubs before but they've been rubbish and I've always been kicked out but this one is the best.'

Jolene Nevin Y5

'I have been coming to After School Club since it started because my mum is one of the helpers. I enjoy the craft activities and when new people start, like Jolene.'

Alex McCormack Y4

What do you think? Add your own comment

Chapter One

There are two parts of my day I don't like very much. The first part is before school; the second part is after school. They're so bouncy since Dad left. I don't mean bouncy like when you're on a bouncy castle and everyone's jumping up and down and bumping into each other and it's a good laugh. I mean bouncy like when you're on a bouncy castle and everyone's jumping up and down and bumping into each other but nobody's in control so you're scared in case you fall off and get hurt. *That* kind of bouncy.

When Dad lived with us, which was until five months ago, I didn't bounce much because I knew where I was. We all did. Ever since I can remember, he would come in from working nights at the furniture warehouse just before Mum started out for work at the knitting factory. He would make us our breakfast, have a chat, take us to school, then go to bed. After school, Dad would collect us, make our dinner, have a chat, wait until Mum got home, have a row with her, then go to work again. So we were never alone. We didn't need childminders or babysitters or nothing.

Now it's all changed and I don't like it one bit. I've told Dad a million times I don't like it and he says all Mum has to do is ask and he'll be back in a blink but she hasn't asked yet and says she never will. I keep hoping she will change her mind because everything's a mess. Take this morning, right? Our kitchen at quarter to eight. It was already feeling bouncy. One reason was Mum wasn't even up yet.

She should have been—she's supposed to set off for work at eight but she'd just kept snoring when I called her earlier. I suppose she's very tired—she was at 'Mingles' with her friend Bridget until one o'clock this morning. Mum and Bridget go to Mingles for Singles three times a week to find Mr Right because neither of them found him first time round.

This time round Mum says her first choice is the actor Ross Clooney because you might as well aim high. She has not had much luck so far, which is good news as far as I'm concerned. The sooner Dad comes back the better, and he doesn't need competition from American film stars.

Another reason I'm feeling bouncy is I'd just asked my two sisters, Gemma and Sasha, to sponsor me for *Children in Need* but they're being really mean about it. 'But it's for little children who haven't got nothing, no clothes or food or nothing,' I said, showing them the cute picture of Pudsey Bear with his little eye bandage on in the corner of my sponsor sheet.

'Little children who haven't got *nothing*?' Sasha tutted. 'It's *anything*, stupid. Haven't you heard of double negatives?'

That's just typical of Sasha since she started at The Magna with Gemma. She began in September and it's only November now but it's as if she's in a secret society or something and sisters still at primary, like me, aren't allowed to join. Still, I'm not one to give up easy, so I tried again. 'Please sponsor me for the children who haven't not got *anything*,' I repeated.

Gemma scowled. She's in Year Nine and does that

a lot. 'What, like we have?' she snapped, combing her fizz-bomb hair over her Coco Pops.

'Spot on,' agreed Sasha. 'They should be fund-raising for us—look at this crud!' She showed me her knife, which had got the last dregs of orange marmalade clinging to it; except it was more green than orange. 'We have to eat mould. Even South American kids in the rainforest don't have to eat mould.'

Then Gemma goes, 'Anyway, like you'll last twenty-four hours without talking,' and Sasha goes, 'Yeah, talk about mission impossible.'

I'd chosen to do a twenty-four hour silence, if you hadn't already guessed. It was either that or a sponsored spell and I'm no good at spelling so I didn't have much choice. Mr Sharkey, my headmaster, is going to shave his head and Mr Idle, my form teacher, is playing a rugby match dressed as one of the Ugly Sisters from *Cinderella*.

4

My ugly sister, Gemma, snatched the sheet off me. 'As I'm feeling generous, I'll give you one p,' she said eventually.

'One p? Wow, thanks!'

'One p *an hour*,' she added, as if that made it any better.

Then Sasha went: 'Put me down for that, too.' Copycat.

'You're both mean,' I told them.

Gemma poked me in the back with the end of her comb. 'I'd rather be mean than fat like you. Look, my comb's disappearing in all that flab. Help! Help!'

'Get off!' I yelled, pushing her away. It wasn't like she had room to talk, neither. I hate our Gemma sometimes, I do.

Luckily we heard Mum clattering down the stairs so Gem backed off and returned to slurping her Coco Pops. There was a gap of a few seconds while Mum slipped into her flat working shoes in the hallway. You can hear the 'plat-plat' sound they make on the cushion flooring. At last she came in looking half asleep and struggling to get her arm through her cardigan sleeve. 'Make me a coffee, someone,' she said, her voice as rusty as an old tin of Whiskas.

'You haven't time, you'll be late,' I pointed out. I knew she mustn't be late. At Pitt's where Mum works with Bridget, they give you warnings. Mum had already had a verbal warning and the next stage was a written warning and after that it was a final warning then you were out.

Mum glowered at the wall clock and sighed. She wasn't going to risk being late again. 'Car keys?'

'Treacle tin,' we chanted.

'Ta.'

She grabbed the keys, grabbed a bag of crisps from the cupboard, and grabbed a two-pound coin out of the dinner money jar. Grab. Grab. Grab. Gemma and Sasha looked at each other, knowing one of them would have to do without lunch if she didn't put it back by Friday. I was all right. I took sandwiches.

I saw Gemma mumble something and grew worried in case she started anything nasty. I hated it when that happened so I thought I'd better say something nice quickly. 'Did Ross Clooney turn up?' I asked.

Mum's face softened immediately. 'No,' she said,

smiling, 'he sent his apologies but he had commitments. He said next week.'

'Aw, never mind,' I said sympathetically, but I was glad really.

'Oh, ple-ase,' Gemma sneered.

'Never mind "ple-ase",' Mum said, her eyes alight. 'For your information there's a Lookalike competition Sunday night and there's going to be a Ross Clooney among them. Even if he's only halfway towards the real thing he'll be worth a bit of a smoochy-woochy, won't he?'

'Oh, puke-a-rama,' we all said and she laughed, puckering up her lips and pretending to kiss him. I sighed with relief because she was so happy and I knew she wouldn't bite my head off when I asked her what was happening after school.

I never know, see. Sometimes it's straight to the childminder, Rosie's; sometimes I come home with Nathan's mum next door and wait until Gemma and Sash call for me; and sometimes I'm allowed to walk back on my own. Oh, except Fridays. Dad always picks me up Fridays. I know where I am one day a week.

We've got an after-school thing called ZAPS After School Club but Mum won't let me go to that. She says it's too expensive even though she hasn't even asked. I wish she would let me go because it looks brilliant. It's in this old mobile hut at the back of the school playground. If you stand right up on your tiptoes you can see through the club's windows and there are craft tables and computers and baskets full of dressing-up clothes and a sweet shop and purple sofas and bean bags. It looks really inviting. The supervisor is a lady called Mrs Fryston who comes into assemblies and tells us what's going on that week at the club.

Mrs Fryston has grey hair but a young face so you can't tell if she looks young for her age or old for her age but whatever she is she's always smiling and seems patient and kind, even when Mr Sharkey teases her and calls the club kids 'the mob in the mobile' and her 'the nut in the hut'.

During the last summer holidays, Mrs Fryston did an 'All the Fun of the Circus' theme and arranged for jugglers and clowns to come in and show everyone how to do tricks and fall over properly. I'd have given anything to have been there that week or any week, but first I had to persuade Mum and that's not easy.

'Where am I after school today?' I repeated.

'What day is it?' Mum said, still in her Ross Clooney dream.

'Wednesday.'

'It's Rosie's then, isn't it?' she sighed. 'Pick you up at half-five-ish. Gotta go.'

Blowing air kisses to no one in particular, Mum turned to leave but I stopped her and reminded her Rosie couldn't do Wednesdays no more because she's got the twins and her spaces are used up.

Mum looked puzzled as if it was news to her, which it wasn't, and took a deep breath in as she tried to fasten her coat. The coat stretched and flattened her boobies. She's big, is Mum; we all are, but she's the biggest. Today, she fills the door frame behind her like a soft green leather mattress with buttons. 'Go to Rosie's anyway. What's she going to do, turn a little girl out in the street?' she said.

I know Rosie won't do that but she'll still be annoyed. Mum already owes her three weeks' money. 'Can't I just come home by myself? I promise not to use the deep fat fryer or answer the door to strangers,' I pleaded.

Mum wasn't having it though. 'No, Sam, not with these dark evenings. Just do as you're told or I get confused. I'm off—make sure you lock up properly and someone put the bin out. See you.'

'See you,' we chorused.

'You are the weakest link, goodbye!' Gemma goes under her breath.

Gemma and Sash left ten minutes after Mum. I was last. I like being last. I like it when the house goes quiet and all I can hear is the ticking of the clock and the noise from the boiler when the pilot light whooshes. I like locking the door and checking it is done properly so no burglars can get in. It makes me feel important.

Chapter Two

I can walk it to school easy. All you have to do is go down to the bottom of Birch Rise, where I live, go past Birch Court where the old people live and then cross over at the bottom by the shops and you're on Zetland Avenue and Zetland Avenue Primary School, ZAPS for short, is at the far end opposite the library. Five minutes tops.

I wouldn't say I loved school, exactly, but it's miles better than home at the moment. In class, I sit with Nazeem Khan, Dwight Baxter, and Aimee Anston on the Yellow Table. They wouldn't be my first choice of partners, to be honest, but we're bunched together right next to Mr Idle's desk at the front because we need the most help. We're all a bit rubbish at things like reading and writing. We're also way behind on merit marks. There's a bar chart behind Mr Idle's desk, showing all the different coloured tables' totals, right? You should see the yellow bar. It's only as high as a postage stamp. Everyone else's look like tower blocks. The trouble is, see, as well as earning them, you can have merit marks taken off you for stuff like talking when it is 'inappropriate', being rude, or not doing homework. That's the main problem on our table—Aimee's rude, Dwight never does his homework, I talk all the time, and Naz does all three. We might start off

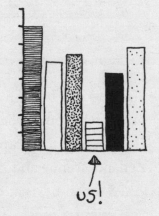

the day with, say, twenty merit marks between us but by home time we can have lost the lot. Mr Idle says we are our own worst enemies.

Anyway, that's the Yellows. When I arrived in class, Aimee was talking about how stupid all this sponsor money thing was. 'I'm not collecting a penny,' Aimee goes, 'it's all a rip-off anyway—the money never gets to the people. The pop stars keep it all.'

Naz pulled a face. 'Yeah, but what about the trip to Radio Fantastico? That's got to be worth two weeks' pocket money, guy.'

Mr Idle knows one of the best presenters at Radio Fantastico—Tara Kitson—and he wangled a slot on her show for us, as part of the radio's Children in Need week. The studios are only small, though, so the whole class can't go, only one tableful. We had a discussion and decided whichever table raised the most money should be the table to go. It was a heated discussion because Sam Riley, who goes to that After School Club I told you about, kept arguing that it wasn't a fair method as the rich kids would win, but not many agreed with him. Sam's usually quiet but he wouldn't back down, even when Aimee said to him, 'So what's your problem? You're a rich kid, aren't you?' His parents own a greetings card shop in the Jubilee Arcade. Sam told her his parents' income was beside the point. Anyway, everyone had a vote and that's the way it went.

Guess what else? Tara Kitson told Mr Idle Radio Fantastico might be linking up live with the *Children in Need* presenters at the BBC but she was not sure when, so there was a chance we might get on telly. Even Aimee couldn't deny she'd like to go on the telly. 'Well, you lot raise the money and I'll come along for the ride,' she sneered. 'Not that we've got a hope, unless Sam takes up stealing again.'

I went bright red. Do you remember Pokemon cards? Well, once, in Year Three, Aimee had dared me to steal some out of the cloakrooms with her or she wouldn't be my friend, so I did. Trouble was, I got caught and she didn't. In fact, she told the teacher she had tried to stop me and they believed her. Aimee is a very good liar. Now she believed it herself and brought it up every so often to make me feel bad. I don't know why she's like that with me. I've never done nothing to hurt her.

Luckily Naz ignored her and said, 'Dwight's got four squids ten and I've got two squids and nought pence and Sam's got—what was it?'

'Thirty pounds,' I said proudly, thinking of all the coins half filling the empty crisp tube on my bedside cabinet. They came from Rosie my childminder and her other mums and going round Birch Court on pension day, which I thought was a stroke of genius. 'Oh, no, wait!' I added, remembering this morning. 'Thirty pounds and forty-eight p.'

Naz nodded wisely. 'Thirty forty-eight. Not bad, guy. But I bet that still means we're well bottom. The Greens have got over fifty and the Reds have got nearly seventy. I don't know about the rest of them but it's gotta be more than us.'

We glanced across the classroom, first to the Red table, then to the Green, then to the rest of them. Everybody beats us Yellows in everything.

'Come on, Anston—you could at least try,' Naz pleaded. 'That Tara is such a babe. She deserves to meet me.'

Aimee finished sharpening a pencil and blew the shavings all over Naz's side. 'Why should I?' she said. 'Nobody makes an effort for me.'

That was such a fib, but never mind—I'm sure

you're getting the picture of what she's like. Then Dwight goes: 'You know Brody Miller in Year Six? She's got over a hundred squid on her own!'

Brody Miller is famous in our school. She's a child model and has been in catalogues and telly adverts and all sorts. If you look in the Argon catalogue on page one hundred and fifteen, she's the one second from the left with the long auburn hair and dazzling smile, sitting on the BMX bike. Not that I'm always looking at her picture, in case you're wondering. She goes to that After School Club as well. It's not fair.

'Well, that's nothing,' I said, glancing at the merit chart, fed up of never getting no recognition for nothing, 'I'll have that easy by Monday.' Don't ask me why I said that because I don't know.

'How?' Aimee goes. 'Your family is always skint. They're not far off being trailer trash, I've heard.'

That really hurt. 'Well,' I said, thinking fast and

fibbing like mad. 'When I got home yesterday, all the residents of Birch Court had done another collection for me—I never asked them or nothing so it was a real surprise—they said they were fond of me and wanted to help. Anyway, that came to—wait for it—fifty pounds.'

'Yes!' Dwight said, punching his fist in the air.

Everyone looked really chuffed, apart from Aimee, who just looked suspicious. I decided to add a bit more. '. . . and then I phoned Dad. I told you he was collecting at the warehouse, right?'

Everyone nodded and I did too because at least that bit was true. 'Well, he told me he's got well over sixty pounds already . . .'

'That's . . .' Naz paused to add up, which he's rubbish at. 'Masses over a hundred. So wicked, Wesley!'

I held my hand up. My mouth hadn't finished yet. I was still stinging from the trailer trash bit. '. . . and he's put a collection box down in The Almighty Cod. You know how busy *that* gets at weekends.' Dad lives above The Almighty Cod now. It's a chip shop on Sandal Road.

Aimee looked at me double-well suspiciously and said: 'You never mentioned that yesterday.'

'I'm not a bragger, Aimee. They don't call me Brody Miller,' I told her, looking her straight in the eye.

'Yellows rock!' Naz grinned, slapping me a high-five.

You won't be surprised to know I was a bit quiet the rest of the morning, wondering what I was going to do. The sponsored silence was on Friday and all the money had to be in by next Wednesday. I'd dropped myself right in it and no messing. I'd just have to come clean at lunchtime, that was all, and put up with all the 'liar, liar, pants on fire' stuff. Aimee would be in her element and get really nasty with me, probably, but I'd just have to take it. I was kind of used to it from her, if you must know.

That was my plan, anyway, until we lined up for assembly and Mr Idle asked us all how we were getting on with our collections. We all muttered, 'Fine', 'OK', 'Not bad'—things like that.

He put out his arm to hold Naz, who was first in line, away from the door frame while the Year Fours trooped past. 'Fine? OK? Not bad?' Mr Idle moaned. 'I want more than that, Year Five! I've got to play rugby dressed in a wig and make-up, not to mention a bikini top stuffed with my wife's old tights. If I'm humiliating myself in front of a crowd of two hundred people, I want "fantastic", "incredible", and "record-breaking", never mind "OK" and "not bad". Understood?'

'Oh, don't get your wife's knickers in a twist, Mr Idle,' Naz goes and everybody laughed.

From further down the line, Sam Riley's voice piped up that he still thought the visit to Radio Fantastico should be made by kids who do something special.

Mr Idle sighed hard. 'We've had this conversation already, Sam, but, for the sake of argument, something special such as?'

'Writing a poem,' Sam said quickly, 'or a catchy verse at least.'

'And I expect you just happen to have one handy?' Mr Idle asked.

'Funny you should mention that,' Sam quipped and everybody laughed. He was quite popular was Sam, though he didn't have one special friend; he just mixed with everybody. I twisted round and could just see the top of his fair head—he's a bit of a titch, height-wise.

'Don't listen to him, Mr Idle,' Aimee called out. 'The table with most money wins it and that's going to be us. Sam Wesley's got way over a hundred pounds all by herself already!' She dug her elbow into my stomach, as if daring me to deny it. Of course, I couldn't then, could I?

Mr Idle beamed at me. Full on, straight in the eyes. 'Is that so, Sam?'

What could I do? Deny it with everybody looking at me? 'Yes,' I said, 'it's true.'

'That's excellent. Well done.'

Aimee winked at me, a massive smirk on her face. She had tricked me into telling another big fat lie and she knew it and she knew I knew it.

Me and my big cake-hole.

Chapter Three

I felt bouncy all afternoon which isn't fair because I don't usually bounce much during school, but I admit it was my own stupid fault this time. Rosie the childminder didn't do much to help the bouncing, neither, when she saw me walking up to her at the gates at half-three. She didn't say nothing to me, exactly, but I could tell by the way she loaded everybody's sandwich boxes into the tray beneath the double-buggy she wasn't happy I was there. I felt treble-bouncy to the point of seasickness all the while I was in her house—as if I didn't have enough to worry about.

When Mum arrived, last as usual, late as usual, Rosie told her straight off she couldn't childmind me no more.

'What's she been up to now?' Mum goes, giving me a deadeye.

'Nothing at all,' Rosie said quickly, 'Sam's a poppet; it's just I want to concentrate on the under-fives.'

'But our Sam's great with little ones. She'd help you, wouldn't you, love?'

I nodded but Rosie had made her mind up. 'Sorry, Eileen, no can do.'

'Fine, fine, I'm not going to beg,' Mum said, clutching my school bag to her chest, and putting on her glum face, 'there's plenty more childminders around.'

'Good luck in finding one that works in arrears,' Rosie said sourly. 'Now, you'll need to pay your fees, please, before you go.'

Mum tried to wriggle out of it. 'I'm short at the moment. Can I post it on?'

'No,' Rosie said firmly, 'you can't.'

She held her hand out and Mum reluctantly pulled out her purse and paid up. It took ages, because she had to scramble about for every last coin she had; then she was forty pence short but Rosie told her to forget about it.

As soon as we got in the car, Mum let rip. 'Oh, that was decent of her, wasn't it? "Forget about the forty p." Stuck up mare . . .'

We set off down the street, Mum ranting on and driving too fast over the speed bumps so I felt my head was going to fall off. 'It's all right for her. She hasn't worked in a factory since she was sixteen, has she, or been married to a loser since she was nineteen? I never had a chance to enjoy myself and let my hair down like I should have done at that age. All I've had is millstones. I'm right, aren't I?'

'Yes, Mum.'

'Millstones' is a Bridget word. She uses it a lot when she telephones. 'Which one of the millstones are you?' she'll say and laugh. I thought it was a compliment at first, like a gemstone, but then Sasha told me what it meant. I don't like Bridget much now. 'That's why I go to Mingles—to catch up on what I've missed out on—it's just for a break and a laugh,' Mum continued.

'I know, Mum. Nobody minds.'

She slowed down behind a queue of traffic at the lights on Batley Road but carried on explaining, even though she didn't really need to. 'I know it's a bit

expensive and I keep telling Bridget I can't keep up with her with clothes and things but, like she says, first appearances count. I'm not going to get Mr Right dressed in seconds from a market stall, am I?'

'No. Why should you? We're not trailer trash, are we?' I agreed quickly, thinking of Aimee's nasty description.

Mum laughed aloud. 'Exactly! We are not trailer trash! Exactly! You're right on my wavelength, Sam. How come you're the youngest but you understand me the most, eh, babe?'

'I don't know,' I said, glowing in her praise. I

paused, then took a chance. 'What's going to happen about me after school now?' I asked.

'Huh . . . I don't know. I'll have to think about it later.'

'I can always go to After School club.'

'What?'

The line of cars moved forward slightly and we nudged nearer the lights. 'After School club—instead of Rosie's. It's really good, Mum. There's themes and a reading corner and a tuck shop . . .' I paused, trying to remember everything I'd heard about it when Mrs Fryston came into assemblies.

'Cut to the bottom line, Sam; how much?'

'I don't know but I don't think it's that much.'

Mum let out a long, deep breath because she knew she had run out of choices. 'What do you do, just turn up?'

'No, you have to fill a form in saying which days you're going to be there and who's picking you up and stuff. Then one of the leaders comes to get you at home time and takes you there.'

'You seem to know a lot about it.'

'I've been observing.'

She sighed hard. 'I suppose you'd better get me one of them form things tomorrow then.'

'OK,' I said, trying not to sound too excited.

At last we got through the lights and headed for home.

The first thing Mum did was go crazy because no one had put the bin out but I didn't mind too much about the shouting because I knew I'd be going to After School club soon and you can stand anything when you've got something good to look forward to, can't you?

Chapter Four

I didn't feel one bit bouncy at school next day. I collected a ZAPS After School Club application form first thing from Mrs Moore, the school secretary, and at break I had a chat to Sam Riley. He looked a bit surprised at first when I walked over to him because we don't mix much. He didn't mind talking about After School club though. He said it was great. He told me he was in charge of the tuck shop and tended to concentrate on that but there were plenty of things to do to suit everyone unless you were a TV freak. 'Mrs Fryston limits that to the last twenty minutes when all the clearing up has been done,' he told me.

'Oh,' I said, 'I'm not bothered. I can watch TV any old time.'

'Exactly,' Sam agreed. He rubbed his chin and stared into the sky. 'Switch the TV off, O Youth of England and Wales . . . It makes your brain go numb and your imagination it jails . . . or fails . . . or—'

'Er . . . very good, Sam,' I interrupted, knowing his poems tended to go into dozens of verses.

'It's a work in progress,' he shrugged, then added, 'You can help me with the tuck shop, if you like. I'm looking for a reliable assistant.'

'Oh, maybe,' I mumbled.

He must have been able to tell I wasn't sure if that's how I wanted to spend my After School club time. I was more into making things. 'You never know, the experience might help you get a job when you're older,' he goes.

'I don't want to work in a shop or a factory!' I told him straight off, thinking of Mum's endless grumbling about Pitt's. 'That would be so boring.'

Sam shook his head at me. 'Oh, you sound just like Luke and Tim—my older brothers—they think that, too. They've told Dad they're not going to work for Riley's when they leave university. Fifty years of tradition gone just like that! I am though. I can't wait until I'm old enough to help out properly and arrange the window displays and serve people and all that. I'm going to design my own range of cards, too. Like Purple Ronnie only different.'

'Oh,' I said, still not convinced.

I guess Sam could tell. He shrugged. 'It has to be in the blood, I suppose.'

I wanted to get back to finding out more about Mrs Fryston but then Naz came up and went, 'Talking to your new boyfriend, Wezz?' and I was forced to chase him across the sandpit to give him a thump and by the time I'd done that the bell had gone and it was mental maths.

Chapter Five

At tea time, Mum agreed to go through my application form with me straight away to get it over and done with before Bridget 'popped in'.

'There,' Mum said, signing her name neatly at the bottom, 'that's you sorted for two hours a day. Now I've just got the other twenty-two to think about!'

'Thanks, Mum, you're the best,' I said happily, leaning across to give her a hug. 'Can I start tomorrow? So I get used to it?'

She shrugged me off. 'If your dad doesn't mind. You know how he is if he misses five minutes with you.'

'I'll phone him now, and ask him, shall I?'

She pulled a packet of cigarettes out of her pocket.

'Ask him if he can pay the first week while you're at it—things are a bit tight for me at the moment.'

'Like that new dress you've got in your wardrobe,' Gemma went.

Dad had just finished having his dinner when I called. Vegetarian goulash. We'd had sausages and oven chips. I told him how Gemma had nearly set the house on fire cooking them. He laughed. 'She'll learn. How was school? Has Aimee been behaving herself?'

He knows sometimes we fall out but I didn't want to discuss Aimee stuff so I began telling him about After School club. He said it sounded 'just the job'. I would have gone into more details but Mum told me to hurry up as money didn't grow on trees. 'Gotta go, Dad. Remember I won't be talking to you tomorrow,' I said.

'OK,' he replied, 'I'll remember. See you at school. Five on the dot. Goodnight, pet.'

'You haven't asked the

question,' I reminded him quickly. He had to ask the question or I wouldn't sleep.

'Oh,' he said, hesitating for some reason, 'erm . . . is she ready to have me back yet? All she has to do is click her fingers . . .' His voice trailed off.

I glanced round, first checking Mum wasn't listening. She didn't know about our little ritual; then I whispered, 'No, but she will, I'm sure. Don't you fret.'

'I won't,' he replied quietly and hung up.

My stomach felt funny straight away. I could have blamed Gemma's sausages but really I knew it was because I always felt funny after I've spoken to Dad. It's because I'm still not really used to him not living with us, if you must know.

Our phone is in the hallway, near the back door. It's where we dump all our stuff as soon as we come in from school. I was just searching in my bag for my maths homework when there was a quick knock on the door and before I had a chance to say, 'Who is it?' Bridget came straight in, bringing the cold with her.

'Hiya, Milly Millstone,' she goes to me, 'is your mum in? I won't be two minutes.'

I scowled at her and followed her through into the

living room. I had wanted to talk to Mum about how I could raise more sponsor money in a hurry but Bridget's arrival had wrecked that. She always said she would only be two minutes but she never was. Two centuries more like. Tonight's two minutes' worth was to ask us what we thought of her new boots.

'Showing off as usual,' Gemma mumbled as we watched her take over.

I don't know what Mum sees in Bridget—she's a bit boring, I think. The only thing that stands out about her is she only takes size three and a half shoes and always wears roll-neck jumpers, even in summer, to hide this birthmark she's got on her neck. It's red and shaped like the Isle of Wight. Other than that she's nothing special.

'What do you reckon?' she goes, moving her tiny feet from one side to the other like a windscreen wiper. The boots were creamy leather knee-highs with a sharp pointy toe and nasty-looking heels.

Gemma and Sasha didn't even glance and just twisted their heads either side of her so they could see the telly but Mum clapped her hands in delight. 'Oh, Bridget, they're gorgeous. How much?'

'I daren't tell you,' Bridget said, then told. It was a lot. A lot a lot.

'Never!' Mum squealed.

'They're Italian—that's what makes them pricey.'

'They are gorgeous,' Mum repeated, her eyes all sparkly. 'What I'd give for a pair of those.'

Bridget smiled tightly and her eyes looked a bit like Aimee Anston's had when she'd told Mr Idle about my imaginary money. A bit shady. 'Well, never mind, Eil, eh?' she smiled. 'Maybe one day when you get rid of the millstones.'

Chapter Six

Next morning was the sponsored silence. I'd started at half-nine when I'd gone to bed so you could say I was already nearly halfway through my twenty-four hours by the time I got to school.

School was easy because I had a perfect excuse not to talk to Aimee. Time dragged a bit, though, I have to admit, until we trooped into the hall to watch Mr Sharkey have his hair shaved off, and then something happened that I had not expected.

A photographer from the *Evening Echo* came and some children had to have a picture taken standing around bald Mr Sharkey. Mr Sharkey asked for teachers to select a pupil from each class and Mr Idle pushed me out before I had chance to mime 'no'.

'Don't forget to say "cheese",' Aimee sniggered.

Guess what? They stood me right next to Brody Miller with her beautiful, long, auburn hair and thick eyelashes and dazzling smile.

I looked straight into the camera, thinking all the time about the crisp tube on my bedside cabinet and how stuffed full of money it was going to be by Wednesday. Somehow, I'd do it. I'd do it for the Yellows and I'd do it for Pudsey. I'd do it, definitely.

Chapter Seven

Before that, though, I had my first experience of After School club. I was really excited when the assistant turned up outside our classroom and felt dead important when she called my name out, then Sam Riley's. She was called Mrs McCormack—I knew that already because her daughter, Alex, is in Year Four and I had seen her loads of times in the playground. I followed quietly behind Sam, first across to Mrs Platini's Year Six class where we picked up Reggie Glazzard but not Brody Miller and then across the playground and over to the mobile on the edge of the playing field.

Sam led the way up the three wooden steps. As we reached the entrance he stood back and said to me:

'*Hope you find that your new home will very quickly bring . . . good luck and happiness to you in simply everything,*' finally adding, 'New Home cards, price band F next to Good Luck and Congratulations.' I rolled my eyes at him to tell him to shut up but he just grinned and pushed open the outer door.

What got me first was how colourful it was inside the mobile. Staring through the dusty windows didn't show you the floor was such a bright green and the walls so bright orange and yellow. It made me blink a few times, I can tell you. The kids who had already arrived had settled quickly. Some were playing board games, some were setting out paints on the craft table and others were just sitting around, chatting. Everything seemed very relaxed. Reggie headed straight for one of the computers.

I couldn't take much more in then because Mrs Fryston was standing by a desk near the inner doorway and Mrs McCormack said she would want to meet me first.

'I'll come with you,' Sam went, 'and act as interpreter.' I felt really grateful when he said that, because he didn't need to—he could have just gone off to his shop.

'Mrs Fryston,' he said grandly to the supervisor, 'can I introduce you to Sam Wesley, a friend of mine. She's on the sponsored silence, so enjoy the peace while you can because normally she never stops talking!'

What a cheek. It was true, though, so I didn't have no right to punch him or nothing. Not that I would anyway, with him being so helpful.

Mrs Fryston looked even nicer close up than she did in assemblies. She had greeny-blue eyes that crinkled kindly at the edges and pretty silver earrings shaped like snail shells. 'I'll just go over your details,' she said, checking through my registration form with me. I had to nod yes or no to her questions. 'Well, Samantha,' she said when she had finished quizzing me about allergies and stuff, 'would you like me to show you round or would you prefer Sam to do it?'

I shook my head vigorously. 'What, you don't want either of us to?' she asked, puzzled.

I shook my head again. 'I don't think she likes being called Samantha,' Sam said. I gave a thumbs up. Gemma and Sasha always called me Samantha-Panther when they were being sarcastic.

Mrs Fryston paused for a second, looking from me to the other Sam. 'Mm. I've got visions of you both shouting "what?" at me when I call out "Sam" though. How about Sammy?'

I nodded. Sammy would do fine.

'With an ie ending, I think,' Sam added.

I nodded again. This boy knew me well.

'Well, then, welcome to Zaps After School Club, Sammie,' Mrs Fryston grinned, and I felt really warm inside.

'Let me show you the shop first,' Sam said, just  about dragging me across the room. 'It's not exactly as I visualize it yet, but I'm getting there.' He guided me towards a wooden market stall with red and white stripy blinds painted down the sides. There was a plastic till and huge tubs full of plastic fruit and vegetables all neatly arranged along the top. 'I'm way behind,' he moaned,  scowling at a plastic pineapple which had a caved-in side before he disappeared beneath a curtain at the back of the stall and started getting out more tubs but full of real sweets this time. There were jelly glow-worms and gummi bears and cola bottles and all sorts. My stomach rumbled just looking at them. He added a pile of small white bags, a felt pen, and a margarine tub float to his goods.

Before Sam had a chance to finish his preparations, a little boy with pink yogurt stains on his sweatshirt wandered over and held out a 10p to me. 'Sweets, please,' he said.

I looked at Sam for guidance. He leaned down towards the boy. 'We're not open for business yet, Brandon, but do come back later. You can do me a favour, though. You can tell everyone we've got a new club member. She's called Sammie. Can you remember that, Brandon?'

Brandon stared at me and nodded. The tiny kid shoved out his bottom lip. 'I only want green ones,' he said to me miserably.

'Later,' Sam repeated. 'We have to have a drink and a biscuit first from over there,' he explained to me, pointing to a tray full of brightly coloured plastic beakers near Mrs Fryston's desk, 'and nobody's allowed more than ten pence worth of sweets in one night.'

'My mummy's just had a baby,' Brandon added.

I smiled as if to say 'that's nice' and he walked off.

'He's one of my best customers,' Sam told me. 'He's a full-timer, like me, so I've got to know him really well. I'm a bit worried about him—he's gone very quiet since his new baby brother arrived.' Sam glanced across at Brandon, who had taken a Spot book from a rack and handed it to a boy on a purple sofa. The boy looked about my age but wasn't wearing a ZAPS uniform. 'That's Lloyd Fountain,' Sam said, following my gaze. 'He's another regular, too. He doesn't go to a school—his parents don't believe in it. Has his lessons with  them at home then comes here to mix with kids his own age.'

I stared in disbelief at Lloyd Fountain. Fancy not having to go to school. I have never heard of that, have you? I know loads of older kids on the estate who don't go to school because they've been excluded but not any that don't go because their parents actually want them at home. I watched as Lloyd's head of curly hair bent over the book he was sharing with Brandon, and saw how he smiled as he pointed out words to him. At least he can read, I thought. If I had lessons at home I bet I wouldn't even know what a book was until I was fourteen. My mum only ever read the TV guide.

Sam shook a tub of cola bottles. 'They stick,' he explained before continuing. 'The only other full-timers are Brody, who's missing today for some reason, Reggie over there, who always hogs the computer unless it's outdoor activities then he hogs the football, and Alex. Alex's a pain,' Sam hissed, as we stared at her squirting orange paint all over an empty Frosties box. 'She hates coming so she makes as big a nuisance of herself as possible. She gets away with so much stuff just because her mum works here. Gets right up my nose.'

I grinned at Sam's serious face.

'What?' he asked.

Glancing round, I took one of the white sweet bags and the felt pen and scribbled, 'And I talk a lot??!!' across the front of the bag.

'Just filling you in on the details,' Sam huffed. 'I haven't even started on the part-timers yet, or the weekly activities. You need to know what's going on, Sammie; you're one of us now, one of the mob in the mobile.'

You probably think I'm being soft, but this glow spread right across my tummy, as if I had just eaten a bowl of creamy porridge. I *was* one of the mob in the mobile, wasn't I? Official.

I scribbled on the bag again. 'YES I AM!! Thanks, Sam.'

That next hour went *so* fast. Sam told me loads more stuff, like how Brody fancied Reggie but Reggie never took his eyes away from the computer long enough to notice and how next time Mr Sharkey 'dropped in' to see Mrs Fryston I had to watch how pink they both went. Sam said he reckoned they were in love which would be cool because Mrs Fryston's first husband had died and she needed a companion. I never knew Mrs Fryston's husband had died. That made me feel really sorry for her, even though it was years ago and she had two teenage daughters and a golden retriever for company.

Do you know what, I think I found out more about people in my school from Sam Riley in an hour than I had in the five years I had been coming here. I couldn't believe it when Dad turned up and it was five o'clock already. He had a bit of a chat to Mrs Fryston and what was nice was everybody waved and said goodbye when I left. After School club was just the best place ever and Sam Riley had a lot to do with that but don't tell him I told you that because I don't fancy him or nothing. I'm not Brody Miller, remember.

Chapter Eight

We caught the bus to Dad's flat and met up with Gemma and Sasha who were already there. They tried teasing words out of me but I still had four hours to go so there was no way I was going to give in to their tricks at this late stage. Not for nothing!

After dinner and an argument about who should get the chair and who should sit squashed up on the bed, because Dad's bed doubled as a sofa, if you know what I mean, we settled down to watch *Children in Need*. At first it was light-hearted and funny but when they showed you short films of where the money was going, we all went a bit quiet. Some of the stories were so sad. One boy called Padraic, who was only my age, had something called arthritis.

Usually it is old people that get it but sometimes you can be born with it, like Padraic. Just walking was agony for him and his finger joints were as big and round as giant marbles.

'That must be horrible to have,' I said. It had gone half-nine so I was allowed to talk again but watching Padraic made me too miserable to celebrate.

'Yeah,' Gemma sniffed gruffly and I looked at her, and she was actually crying, but she gave me a deadeye so I looked away pronto.

'Hey, shall we see how much I collected from work for you?' Dad goes. 'I think we did OK.'

'Yeah,' I said eagerly, 'quick—let's count it now!'

Dad grinned and went to the kitchen unit opposite us to find the collection. My heart leapt as he dropped the box in my lap. For one wild second I thought wouldn't it be great if he had collected so much money he had solved all my problems *and* Padraic's? But I knew as soon as I felt the weight of the box that wouldn't be happening and I was right—it was nowhere near. The warehouse collection came to a crummy eight pounds and seven pence and loads of pesetas. 'Well, I don't know who put those in!' Dad said, holding up the foreign silver coins.

'How much are they worth?' Gemma asked.

'Nothing—Spain has euros now. Never mind, here,' he said, digging into his trouser pocket, 'pocket money time. Don't spend it all at once.'

'Give mine to Pudsey,' Gemma said.

'Mine too,' Sasha added.

'You're not kidding me, are you?' I asked but I knew from their faces I wasn't the only one who felt bad for Padraic.

'Well, if we're being charitable, I'd better add my pocket money, too,' Dad went, and handed me a five-pound note which was the same amount he gave us.

'Can't you do better than that?' Sasha asked.

'No,' Dad smiled, 'I need some for myself. I'm going to the pictures on Sunday.'

'Oooh—hot date, eh, Dad?' Gemma teased.

As if he would. She said such thick things sometimes.

'Er . . . how much will that be you've raised, Sam?' Dad asked quickly.

I mentally added the twenty to the rest in the crisp tube at home. 'Erm . . . about fifty pounds,' I said. There was no point fibbing to him.

'That's fantastic!' Dad said, his eyes all shiny and proud and I thought, any other time, it would have been.

I felt a bit miserable the rest of the night and only got to sleep by imagining I was at After School club chatting to Sam and helping him serve out gummi bears.

Chapter Nine

Mum was already leaving for Mingles when we got home on Sunday, even though it was only seven o'clock. 'I'm going early to get a seat at the front,' she explained, peering into the hallway mirror to check her lipstick. 'There's some sausage rolls and coleslaw in the fridge and I've bought you a big bar of chocolate each, as a treat.' She seemed over-excited and in a bit of a rush. Gemma and Sasha just barged past her without really speaking but I hovered round, wishing she wasn't going out so soon. I hadn't seen her since Friday morning and had stacks to tell her. I knew she'd be fascinated about Mrs Fryston being a widow and Lloyd Fountain having lessons at home, not to mention Padraic's fingers.

I watched as she pressed her lips together over a folded tissue; that's a trick to seal the lipstick, apparently. 'How do I look?' she asked.

She was wearing the new black dress that clung tightly everywhere. It was cut low, so you could see her boobs wobbling out over the top like half-set jellies. On her legs she wore black, shiny tights which looked nice until you got to the battered work shoes on her feet. I thought they didn't really go and I said so, thinking I was being helpful. 'I'll fetch you your black suede ones if you want. They'd be better, I think.'

It also meant a few more seconds with her while I fetched them downstairs, but I got a fierce look and I knew I'd said the wrong thing.

'The heels are too high on those. Men don't like it if you're taller than them,' she snapped.

'Oh, I didn't know that. Sorry. You look really gorgeous anyway,' I told her quickly. 'That Ross Clooney will take one look at you and think "Cor, what a babe!"'

Her eyes sparkled. 'Oh, give up!'

'He will. You're really pretty, Mum. You don't need new boots to get noticed.'

'What's that supposed to mean?' Mum said, flicking her eyes over me for a second before snatching her coat from the hook.

My heart sank as I knew I had said the wrong thing again. 'Nothing. I just meant . . .'

But that was it, she was off, one hand on the door, one fastened round her lilac clutch bag leaving her nothing free to hug me with. 'Don't stay up late, you've got school tomorrow,' she called, banging the door behind her.

'I know—and After School club,' I called after her but she was gone.

In the front room, Gemma was watching telly and Sasha was doing her homework at the table so I went upstairs to get my stuff ready for school and put my sponsor money all together. Guess what? When I got to my bedroom, the empty crisp tube was missing from my bedside cabinet. Ha, ha, Sasha, I thought.

I quickly changed into my pyjamas and went downstairs. 'It's not funny, you know,' I go to Gemma and Sasha, 'in fact it's dead boring.'

'What is, your face?' Gemma mumbled.

'You know what I mean,' I said.

She reluctantly tore herself away from the television screen. 'What do you want, pain-in-the-neck?' she went.

'Hiding my crisp tube. So mature.'

'I haven't seen it!'

'Me neither,' Sasha said, before I'd even asked her. 'Gem, tell me why Galileo was important to science.'

How dense did they think I was? They were always teasing me and I was fed up with it. Especially this time; hiding someone's sponsor money was way over the line. 'Give it back, now, or I'll phone Dad,' I shouted. I meant it, too.

Gemma scowled. 'Dad's going out, remember? And we haven't touched your stupid money! We haven't have we, Sasha?' Sasha shook her head. I waited for the secret look to pass between them but it never happened.

'Where is it then?' I asked. My eyes stung with tears but I didn't care if they saw them or not. It was all right for them. They hadn't told a massive lie about how much they had collected. I knew my collection wasn't much but I had to have something to hand in or I'd look a complete liar. 'I hate you two!'

I yelled at them. 'Just because I'm the youngest you think you can do what you want. Well, you can't. Now give me my crisp tube or I'm phoning Dad and if he's not there, I'm calling the police!'

Sasha pushed herself back on her chair and stared at me in amazement. 'Nobody's touched your precious money!'

'Where is it then?'

Tossing down the remote control, Gemma stomped out of the room. 'It'll be exactly where you left it, you big fat cry-baby,' she called, pounding up the stairs. I raced after her, thinking she'd go straight to wherever she had hidden it and pretend she had just happened to find it, but she didn't. Gemma looked in all the same places I had already looked—under the bunk beds, behind the curtains, the back of the wardrobe—everywhere.

Finally, I believed her. She seemed as hot and bothered as I was. I remembered she had given me her pocket money and she had cried at Padraic's fingers, too. I had to think of other solutions. 'Maybe Mum took it into her room for safe-keeping,' I suggested.

Gemma looked at me, then looked across the hallway at Mum's closed bedroom door. 'Yeah,' she agreed, 'maybe she did—it wouldn't surprise me.' For some reason, she sounded angrier than me.

Mum's room was a total mess. There were clothes piled everywhere like in a jumble sale—all over her bed, her chair, her wardrobe door. Gemma ignored all that and dived straight under the bed.

'Aha!' she grunted after a few seconds.

'What is it?' I asked, squatting down to see what she was 'aha-ing' at. Gemma was pulling at a large

white box which had been shoved right back against the wall. Bit by bit, she edged the box out from under the bed, bringing dust and fur balls and screwed-up tissues with her.

'What is it?' I asked again.

'A shoe box, dummy. What do you think it is?' she went, then sneezed.

'So? It's a crisp tube we want.'

'Look at the picture on the side.'

I looked. It was a picture of knee-high boots with pointy toes. 'Why's Bridget left that here?'

'Sam, you're so thick sometimes,' Gemma went but she didn't say it nastily.

'What do you mean?'

'Look at the size of the boots—a seven.'

'So?'

'Do I have to spell it out? Mum's used your money to buy new boots just so she can keep up with Bridget the Widget. It's so obvious.'

'The boots cost way more than I collected,' I went, remembering what Bridget had quoted.

'OK, then put it towards them, then!'

'She wouldn't do that.'

But Gemma wasn't listening. Instead, she flicked up the shoe box lid and let out a long, deep breath. 'Look,' she said, 'now will you believe me?'

I looked. There it was, my crisp tube, surrounded by white tissue paper and totally, totally empty.

Chapter Ten

I didn't sleep much and neither did Mum, judging from the tired way she dragged herself into the kitchen the next morning. She snapped as upright as a newly placed lamp-post in cement, though, when she saw the shoe box in the middle of the table. 'What's that doing here?' she goes, dead angry, looking at each one of us in turn.

I turned to Gemma for help. She had warned me Mum would get all defensive but we had to stand firm. To show me how, she set-to immediately. 'Good question!' Gemma yelled, sticking her chin out defiantly.

'I don't have time for this,' Mum yelled back.

'Make time, Mum. This is important,' Sasha went, dead calm compared to Gemma.

And definitely calm compared to Mum, whose face had gone the colour of cranberry sauce. Even for her, the shouting was way over-the-top. 'Important? I'll tell you what's important—respect! I walk into my own kitchen for a simple cup of coffee and this is what I get—the third degree. Nobody's even asked me how last night went. My big night!'

'How did it go?' I said. Gemma threw me a warning look not to get sucked into distractions but I couldn't help it. It's just the way I am.

'Awful!' Mum wailed. 'Just awful! I bought Ross Clooney drinks all night and then right at the end, when I went to get my coat, he disappeared without a word! The pig!' Mum cried. 'And his real name was Dave Brighouse. Dave Brighouse! That's not very romantic, is it, even for a lookalike?'

Her cheeks wobbled as if preparing for wet conditions but Gemma wasn't having any of that.

 'Who cares? Mum, we know you've been over-spending again—we've found the empty crisp tube,' Gemma said but this time there was no anger in her voice, neither, just hurt and disappointment. 'How could you, Mum? Our Sam's sponsor money? How could you? That is so low.'

Tears sprang into Mum's eyes and she fumbled immediately into her pocket for a hanky. She started crying then and I couldn't stand it. 'Don't, Mum, don't!' I pleaded, dashing round the table and wrapping my arms round her. Her shoulders were juddering but she still managed to hug me back.

'I just borrowed it, Sam, to buy food with . . . you'd have had nothing to eat otherwise . . . those nice chocolate bars . . . I couldn't let you starve, could I?'

'Why didn't you have any money left? You get paid, don't you?' Gemma pressed.

Mum glanced towards the hallway. 'When I bought the boots . . .'

'Aha!' Sasha cried like one of those lady solicitors in court.

Game up, Mum took a deep breath and started to explain. 'When I bought the boots, they maxed out my banker's card so it wouldn't work in the Co-op— you just don't know how embarrassing that was— that snotty Rosie Redfern was stood right behind me

. . . so I came home and remembered the sponsor money and . . . I borrowed it.'

She took my arm. 'I'm sorry, Sam, I wouldn't have done it if it hadn't been an emergency, you know I wouldn't.' Huge tears were rolling uncontrollably down her cheeks and I felt really sorry for her. Sorry and a bit cross, if you must know, but mostly sorry. 'I . . . I just wanted to feel extra special . . . in something new for Ross Clooney. Bridget says you should always buy something new to wear for an important date . . .'

'But it wasn't even a date and the guy dumped you anyway after he'd cadged off you all night,' Gemma said in frustration. 'Mum, you're such a loser. A total and absolute loser.'

'I know,' Mum admitted, 'I know.'

I slipped away then, leaving the house first for once. I didn't want to be there any more.

Chapter Eleven

It was cold outside but I didn't mind. I walked slowly to school, keeping my head down, trying to work things out. But I couldn't. I kept trying but I couldn't. Every time I had one thought about the money it bumped into another one about Mum and got tangled; like those line mazes where you have to trace your pencil along a route to find your way out but all you find is dead ends and in the end you give up and scribble all over the page in frustration. That's how my mind felt as I crossed Zetland Avenue and got nearer to school—like thousands of dead ends with Mum crying at me from some of the ends and Aimee Anston leering at me from the rest.

By the time we were allowed in for registration, I felt really poorly. Being early, I was at the front of the line when I began swaying. 'Are you OK?' Mr Idle asked worriedly. Next thing I knew, I was in Mrs Moore's office with my head between my knees.

'What happened?' I said.

Mrs Moore told me I'd nearly fainted.

'Oh. I've never done that before,' I said. I tried to look up but everything was still fuzzy.

'You look very pale to me,' Mrs Moore goes. 'I've tried calling your mum at work but they say she hasn't turned up yet. Have you any idea where she might be?'

'No. She's always late.'

'You'd be better off at home, pet.'

'I don't want to go home,' I wept.

Mrs Moore passed me
a tissue. 'Would you
like a friend to come
and sit with you then?
Aimee or someone?'

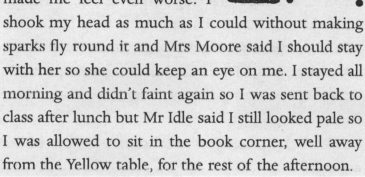

The thought of Aimee
made me feel even worse. I
shook my head as much as I could without making
sparks fly round it and Mrs Moore said I should stay
with her so she could keep an eye on me. I stayed all
morning and didn't faint again so I was sent back to
class after lunch but Mr Idle said I still looked pale so
I was allowed to sit in the book corner, well away
from the Yellow table, for the rest of the afternoon.

At half past three, Mrs McCormack came to
collect the After School kids and for the first time that
day I cheered up. 'You've recovered all of a sudden,'
Aimee said as I hurried past her. 'That's good—you'll
be able to bring all your money in tomorrow, won't
you?'

I pretended I hadn't heard.

As soon as I set foot in the mobile, I felt calm. Don't
ask me why. All the fuzz in my head just cleared
instantly. Maybe it was because I knew that for two

hours I was free. Aimee wasn't here to bug me. Mum wasn't here to confuse me. Gemma wasn't here to stir up trouble. Here I was someone I wanted to be. Here I was Sammie and I didn't bounce.

There were more kids at the club this time, so it was a bit noisier and a bit busier. Brody Miller was there, too. I kept glancing across at her, watching what she did. Sam had asked me to help him in the tuck shop again, so I had a good view of her. Don't ask me why, but I was kind of interested in Brody Miller; she was the nearest I had ever been to a famous person.

'Don't tell me you're another Brody Miller admirer?' Sam said.

'What do you mean?'

'You've done nothing but goggle at her for the past twenty minutes. She's ordinary underneath it all, you know. She slurps her spaghetti and burps like the rest of us—believe me. I've had to sit opposite her in Piccollino's often enough.'

'How come?' I asked. Piccollino's is a posh Italian restaurant in town. Mum and Bridget go there sometimes.

Sam shrugged. 'My parents are friends with hers. Mrs Miller exhibits her ceramics in our gallery—you know, the one above the shop? Mum and Dad have got friendly with her.'

I just said, 'Oh, right, course,' as if exhibiting things in galleries was normal in my family, too.

'And Brody bores for England when she gets talking about Reggie. "Oh, Reggie. Oh, Reggie!" Oh, puke,' Sam grunted.

'She is pretty, though, isn't she?' I went, still staring.

'No prettier than you,' Sam said.

I looked at him to see if he was being funny but he just shrugged. 'Well, she isn't,' he continued, 'it's just that she's got her own personal hair stylist and nail stylist and bogey stylist . . . Besides, her good looks haven't helped her get Reggie to notice her, have they?'

Reggie, as usual, was hammering away on the computer keyboard. 'Shh!' I said, giggling. 'She's coming over.'

'Get your autograph book out.'

'Stop it!'

Brody was first in line with Brandon and Lloyd. 'Hi, Sam, hi, Sam,' she said, ever so friendly.

'It's Sammie,' I said shyly, 'to tell us apart.'

'Oh,' she said and smiled, 'cool.' Her teeth were white and even, I noticed. It didn't stop her having her share of sweets, though. I wouldn't have thought

models were allowed. Brody Miller chose cola bottles and cherry lips. She said 'coh-ler' for cola, like Americans do.

'Ten p, please, Brody,' Sam said in his professional manner.

'And whatever these guys want,' she said, indicating her fans. The two boys said 'Thanks' and smiled at her as if she was a princess.

While they were choosing, Brody took out this purse from a small leather duffel bag. The purse was really pretty—made out of a pink shiny fabric and decorated with sparkly beads and large round mirror-like sequins. I wished I had one like that. She couldn't open the zip at first, though, and she had to tug really hard. 'Oh, my sponsor money keeps getting stuck in the zipper,' she said frowning.

'Haven't you handed it in yet?' Sam asked.

'I kept forgetting. I was late this morning, then Mrs Moore wasn't in the office when I went to put it in the safe at lunchtime . . . you know what it's like.'

Sam tutted. 'You should give it to Mrs Fryston— she'll look after it. You've raised hundreds, I've heard.'

Brody rolled her big blue eyes. 'Oh, the rumour mill's been working overtime again. Not hundreds— hundred—one hundred. Period.'

'It's still a lot. You shouldn't be carrying it around,' Sam told her.

Brody tugged at the purse zip, easing it open bit by bit. 'I will when I get the darned thing open—the plastic bag's caught. Hey, success!'

Finally, she held up a two-pound coin and presented it to Sam.

'I haven't got enough change, yet,' Sam said, shuffling a few 10 p's about in the tub.

'Oh, keep it,' she goes, breezily chewing on a cherry lip.

'Will you play dressing-up with us, Brody?' Brandon asked. I saw he was still wearing the sweatshirt with the yoghurt stains down the front.

'Sure, in a second—you go find something classy,' Brody said, then turned to me. 'Hey, our picture should be in the *Echo* tonight. Fifty p says it will be really gross—that guy didn't have a clue, did he?'

What did she have to bring that up for? I'd been really relaxed until then.

'How did you do it?' she asked.

'What?'

'Raise the cash?'

'Erm . . . I went round . . . collecting.'

A pained look crossed Brody Miller's face and she pressed her hand on my sleeve. I stared down at her nails which were painted dark blue with transfers of white daisies perfectly placed in the centre of each one. 'Oh, I knew it!' she goes. 'You make me feel so bad. I bet you spent hours out in the rain, collecting door to door . . .'

'Well,' I began.

'I feel such a fraud!' she continued quickly. 'India Hevlyn—you know—she's in the Gap Christmas advert—India and me just donated our fees for stomping up and down the catwalk for, like, half an hour at the NEC last week. Is that cheating?'

'Er . . . no . . . you still earned it,' I said.

Her eyes lit up and she smiled widely at me. 'Oh, thanks. People get the wrong idea about me sometimes, you know . . .'

Before she could tell me what sort of wrong ideas, Sam said, 'Does Jake know you've given it all to charity?'

Brody held her daisy nail up to her lip and flung back her hair. 'Really, darling—do you think I'm mad? Kiersten knows though, but shush, OK?'

'Who's Jake, who's Kiersten?' I asked when Brody had gone to the dressing-up area.

As usual Sam was only too glad to fill me in on the details. 'Her parents. Jake Miller, her father, owns Miller's Models and Kiersten Tor's her mother who used to be a top catwalk model but now paints and sculpts. Kiersten's really nice but Jake's a bit tight-fisted. That's why I asked Brody  about the sponsor money—I knew she wouldn't have told him what she'd done—he never gives to charity. I think that's wrong, don't you? If you have wealth you should give some back.'

'Oh, sure,' I sighed, not thinking about that but thinking if I called my mum Eileen or my dad Vaughan I'd get well told off for being cheeky.

'Do you want to join her?'

'Who?' I asked.

'Brody. You don't have to help me every time you come to After School club,' Sam said.

I glanced across at Brody Miller laughing as she fitted a straw hat on to Brandon's small head. He was already wearing a dress fifty sizes too big for him and carrying a pink patent handbag. Lloyd had found a man's oversized tweed jacket and pair of high heels. They reminded me of Bridget's boots. 'No, I'll stay here if that's OK with you.'

Sam looked pleased. 'Good. I like reliability and loyalty in my assistant managers.'

I managed a grin. You can't not with Sam, even if you don't know what he is talking about half the time.

Chapter Twelve

No guesses for who was last to be picked up. Little me, of course. Apart from Alex, that was, who didn't count because she had to be there because her mum worked there. By ten past six, even they had left and I was alone with Mrs Fryston.

I decided to help Mrs Fryston tidy away the dressing-up clothes. 'I bet my mum's forgotten and gone to my old childminder,' I explained. I knew she wouldn't but I felt I had to come up with something.

Mrs Fryston gave me a quick smile as if to say 'it's not your fault'. 'Oh, no worries. I've got to stay late for a meeting with Mr Sharkey anyway.' She smiled again and patted me on the hand. 'Can I leave you to finish this? I need to make a phone call.'

'Sure.'

And that's when I found it. Brody's purse. Lying between a tangerine coloured silk underskirt and the tweed jacket. I could see the edge of the plastic bag containing her one hundred pounds sponsor money caught again in the zip.

Without a second's thought, I slipped it into my pocket and carried on tidying up, intending to give it to Mrs Fryston when she came off the phone. But then Mum arrived, and I knew straight away she was upset, so I just waved goodbye to Mrs Fryston and left. I forgot all about the purse. I really did, especially when I looked at Mum properly under the glare of the cloakroom light.

'Are you all right, Mum?' I asked her as she moved from one foot to the other as if her feet were on fire.

'I'll tell you outside,' she said. 'Wrap up warm, it's windy.'

She didn't speak again until we were reversing out of the car park. 'I've had a nightmare day . . .' she goes. 'First off I get that thing.' I followed her gaze to a brown envelope sticking out of the glove compartment. 'A written warning about bad timekeeping from Pitt's. Bridget got one, too. Can you believe it?'

I could believe it, but didn't say nothing, just listened. 'Sixteen years I've worked there and that's all the thanks I get . . . wouldn't listen when I tried to explain I had to return those boots this morning because the shop closed half day—how was I to know it didn't even open until half nine? On top of that, I couldn't get a refund—scuffed them, they said. Then, to cap it all, I find out your dad's seeing someone,' she goes, 'a woman he met at work. Can you believe it?'

My heart pounded like hail on a glass roof. 'No,' I replied, 'I can't. You must be wrong.'

She scowled and indicated left. 'That's what I said. "How can he find someone before I do, with his lousy dress sense?" I said, but I've heard it from more than one person, so it must be true. Julie, she's called.'

'Well, you'd better tell him to come back quick, then, before it gets serious. All you have to do is click your fingers, remember,' I told her sharply.

She glanced at me and I could tell she changed whatever she was going to say. What she did say was bad enough. 'I don't want him back, babe. Not now, not ever,' she goes, 'so get used to it.'

I remembered Brody's purse again when I was getting into my pyjamas and remembered again when I felt it the next morning as I got ready for school. I know what you are thinking and you're dead wrong. I never planned to keep the money. I had enough to think about with the boots business and this Julie person, didn't I? No, I planned to hand the purse straight in and I would have done, too, if it wasn't for Aimee Anston and her nasty mush.

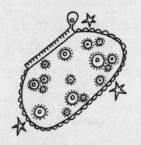

Chapter Thirteen

This is what happened, right? After register Mr Idle reminded everyone about tomorrow being the last day to bring in the sponsor money. He looked at his list and said so far we had a class total of two hundred and sixteen pounds with the Green Table having raised the most with eighty-nine pounds. The Greens cheered their heads off.

'Who's raised the least?' Dwight shouted out. 'Apart from lazy Aimee!'

Mr Idle shot Dwight a dirty look but it wasn't half as withering as the one Aimee fired at him. 'It doesn't matter who's raised the least, Dwight, it's the joint effort that counts,' Mr Idle said.

'Does the top table still go on the radio, though?'

'Yes. It's all arranged for Friday afternoon. Mr Sharkey is going to cover for me while I drive the winners to Radio Fantastico, so the sooner we have all the money in, the sooner I'll know who'll be going.'

Naz sat back and rocked on the back legs of his chair. 'Well, when Sam hands her money in, that's going to be us. Will I be able to tell Tara Kitson my joke about the monkey and the liquidizer?'

'I haven't heard it but I can categorically say definitely not, Nazeem,' Mr Idle goes, then switched his attention to me. 'Nice picture of you in the paper, Sam.'

My stomach plunged a thousand metres. 'I didn't see it,' I said.

Aimee snorted loudly.

'There's no need for that silly noise, Aimee,' Mr Idle said tersely. He hated silly noises.

Aimee scowled at him. She hated being told off. 'She en't got it, so I don't know why you're making such a fuss of her. She wouldn't even have been in the paper if it wasn't for me,' Aimee told him before turning to Naz and Dwight. 'She en't got it, so don't go dreaming of being on radio or telly cos it en't going to happen.'

'What are you talking about?' Mr Idle asked sharply. Between you and me, I don't think he liked Aimee that much either, but being a professional, he wasn't allowed to show it.

Aimee stared coolly at me as if to say 'Your time's up, buddy', then folded her arms and said to Mr Idle: 'The money. She en't got it. She en't collected a penny, just like me, only I en't lied about it.'

Naz leaned across the table and punched Aimee in the arm. 'She has—so shut your cake-hole!'

Aimee thumped him right back, equally as hard. 'No, she hasn't. She's made it up. Ask her before she pretends to faint again!'

There was a pause that felt as heavy as a sack of potatoes pushing into my back. Naz and Dwight looked daggers at her, then me, daring me to tell them Aimee was wrong.

So I did. 'I have got it! I'll get it now!' I burst out. I stood up and walked straight out of the classroom. I know you can guess what I did next but leave me alone. I bet you're not perfect, either.

In the cloakroom, I rummaged deep into my school bag. First I brought out the bit of money I did have—the warehouse collection and the pocket money that were all jumbled together in an old margarine tub—then I rummaged again. From beneath my PE socks, I pulled out Brody's purse, remembering to be careful with the zip as I opened it. I nearly did faint again as I plucked out the neat roll of notes: a fifty, two twenties, and a ten. I had never seen a fifty-pound note before but I knew I didn't have time to gawp, so I crumpled each of the notes up to make them look a bit used and more like Dad's tatty fiver and mixed them in with the coins which still included the pesetas I'd left in for bulk. Finally, I patted down the lid and returned to the classroom.

My heart was hammering away in my chest as I pushed open the door. I felt so angry. Angry with every one of the Yellows for making me do this; angry with Brody Miller for leaving her purse for me to find; angry with Mum for buying those stupid boots; and angry with Dad for going out with someone from work called Julie and not telling me. Most of all, I was angry with me.

I stalked across to Mr Idle's desk and slammed the tub down on top of his pile of marking. 'Here you are, sir. One hundred and thirty pounds, more or less. Watch out for the pesetas!'

'Potatoes? What potatoes?' Naz goes.

'You'd better check it's not come from a Monopoly box!' Aimee fought back but you could tell she was well miffed at the sight of the money.

Mr Idle quickly peered into the tub and smiled. 'No, definitely not Monopoly money. Well done, Sam. And Aimee, I'll see you at break—I don't like your attitude.'

'Who cares? I don't like yours that much, either!' she answered back, going one step too far, as usual.

That meant she was straight to Mr Sharkey's office for the rest of the day and all I had to worry about was facing Brody Miller at After School club.

Chapter Fourteen

The first thing I saw when I walked into the mobile was Brody talking to Mrs Fryston. Brody wasn't crying or nothing, so that was good, but she did look a bit miserable and kept shrugging her shoulders when Mrs Fryston asked her something.

I was prepared for the worst. Any minute now, Mrs Fryston was going to come over to me and question me. As soon as she did, I would tell her everything. It would be a relief, to be honest.

Still, I kept my head down and followed Sam to the cupboard where the sweets were stored, thinking I might as well do something until everything went pear-shaped. 'Is it OK if I help you set up?' I asked.

'Sure,' he said, passing me a tub of flying saucers. 'You put these out and I'll tidy the stock cupboard— it's disgusting. I never get the chance usually but I've got you now.'

He said it in such a taking-for-granted-we'll-always-work-together way. I can't tell you how sad that made me feel.

Mrs Fryston was over at the dressing-up corner now, talking to Brandon and Lloyd. They were both shaking their heads and looking at Brody sorrowfully. Lloyd said something and began taking clothes out of the basket and Brandon joined in, too, thinking it was a game. He began laughing and scattering clothes all over the place until Lloyd put a hand on his arm and calmed him down. At least he's cheerful today, I thought. Finally, it happened. Mrs Fryston and Brody slowly made their way towards the stall.

My heart raced. I felt sick and shaky.

'Sam,' Mrs Fryston goes. We both looked up. 'Sammie,' Mrs Fryston goes, focusing on me, 'do you remember seeing Brody's purse yesterday?'

'Yes,' I mumbled, clinging hard to the plastic container, 'it was pretty—with sequins.'

'I lost it,' Brody said, rolling her eyes. 'Dumb, huh?'

'Can you remember seeing it when you were

tidying the dressing-up clothes last night?' Mrs Fryston asked. 'It's got all Brody's sponsor money inside.'

I opened my mouth to speak, to tell her everything, but nothing came out.

Sam answered instead, 'Oh, Brody, you nit! I told you.'

Brody scowled right back at him. 'Don't bust my chops, Riley. I've already heard it from Mom and Mr Sharkey and Mrs Platini and the world.'

'Well, I did tell you,' Sam repeated.

Mrs Fryston was more patient. 'Where did you last see it, Brody? Can you remember?'

Brody looked fed up, as if she was tired of repeating the same answer. It was a surprising answer though. She sighed heavily and went, 'Well, I'm kind of sure I had it when I left here—I think I remember putting it in my bag as Kiersten collected me. I'm ninety-nine per cent sure I dropped it in the car. I always kind of just dump everything on the back seat when I get in, you know? Kiersten was going to clean it today and phone school if it turned up; she already phoned Piccollino's where we had dinner but nothing was handed in there. Like she said, it could be anywhere. I'm such a Nelly No-brain.'

Anywhere? Nelly No-brain? My heart started thumping against my chest. Brody was blaming herself! She didn't suspect me at all and neither did Mrs Fryston, judging by the look on her face.

'Oh dear,' Mrs Fryston went, giving Brody a quick hug, 'it's such a pity. Well, we'll all have a thorough look in here anyway—you never know.' Without warning, Mrs Fryston clapped her hands together loudly, making me drop the tub of sweets, and asked everyone to listen. As I scrambled after the rolling flying saucers, she explained about the sponsor money and told everyone to have a really good look. While we began the hunt, Brody drew a diagram of her purse on the whiteboard, labelling it with funny captions like: 'Help me, I'm lost' and 'Cranky zipper'

and 'Gunge from squashed jelly belly beans bottom right'.

'See how seriously she's taking it,' Sam muttered. 'Easy come, easy go.'

I didn't say a thing. I held my breath, thinking the longer I kept quiet, the longer I could stay with Sam. I knew I shouldn't. I knew I should have told the truth, but when Brody said, 'I'm sure I had it when I left,' it was like God or someone was saying, 'I'm letting you off this time, Samantha Wesley, seeing as you've got enough to worry about with that mother of yours and that Aimee and that new Julie woman BUT DON'T DO IT AGAIN!!!!' That's what I told myself, anyway. Your mind can tell you anything you want it to when it's desperate enough. Sometimes, you believe it.

Chapter Fifteen

I believed it when I got up the next morning, too. Guess what Mum had done for us all? Only made a cooked breakfast, with waffles and beans. We usually only ever had that on a Sunday. 'Did you hear that?' Mum chirped, turning up the volume on the radio, '*Children in Need* has raised the most it's ever raised. That's good news, isn't it?'

'Yeah,' Gemma goes, 'no thanks to you.'

I shot her a dirty look. Trust her to start spoiling things.

'Don't start,' Mum said, glancing quickly at Gemma then focusing on me, 'I've said I'll pay it back and I will, won't I, babe?'

I was tempted to tell her it didn't matter, that it was

all sorted out, but of course I couldn't, so I just said 'Yep,' and swallowed my last piece of waffle. Mum nodded at me then plodded into the hallway to get ready for work. Coat on, keys in hand, and still only twenty to eight; Mum really was taking her written warning seriously.

Before she left, she stuck her head round the kitchen door, then hesitated. 'Er . . . Bridget's asked if I want to go to the karaoke with her tonight. Would that be all right with you lot?'

Gemma stared at Sasha who stared at me who stared at Mum. This was another turn up. Asking permission to go out. 'OK,' we chorused. Maybe, just maybe, I thought to myself, this whole thing happened to make Mum into a better Mum.

'Thanks, babes. I was going to stay in but like Bridget says, I can't afford to spend time with my millstones when all the good men are being snapped up fast. See you!'

Well, it was a start.

I took my plate over to the sink. Gemma came up and stood next to me. 'So you know about Julie?' she goes.

'Sort of,' I mumbled, scowling at her. From the

way she asked I could tell she had known for ages. Typical. Always the last to know everything, me.

'Dad would have told you but he was worried about how you'd react,' she said as if she could see into my head.

'I don't care,' I shrugged. 'It's his business, not mine.' Angrily I rinsed my plate under the cold tap, shooting water everywhere, thinking maybe she'd get the hint I didn't want to talk about him and stupid Julie. OK, I did really. 'He should have said, that's all. I'm not a baby. It wasn't fair to keep pretending,' I mumbled.

'That's what we told him,' Gemma goes, turning the tap off before I flooded everything.

'She sounds nice,' Sasha added, as if it would help. 'She collects old teddy bears.'

'I'm not ready for details,' I said quickly. 'I have to get used to him not coming back first.'

'Yeah,' Sasha sighed, 'that does take the longest. I still miss not kissing him before I go to school. It was my good luck kiss.' That surprised me, that did.

'I miss the rows,' Gemma added, surprising me even more. 'They did my head in, but at least it meant they were both home!'

I waited, expecting her to follow up with

something sarky but she didn't. 'Maybe we could talk about it tonight, while Mum's out?' I suggested.

I thought they'd say no way, they had better things to do than chat with little brats like me but they agreed straightaway. 'My room, half-seven,' Gemma goes. 'Bring biscuits.'

After they'd left, I made my sandwiches and wiped down the table. I listened to the boiler go whoosh and packed my bag. Everything was quiet and peaceful. As I locked the door behind me, I realized I was looking forward to coming home and being with my sisters.

The bouncing started as I headed for school. It was funny, that, because it was usually the other way round. I told myself it was because Mr Idle was announcing the Radio Fantastico winners today. That meant I wasn't bouncing, really, I was just nervous and sometimes it was hard to tell the difference. It had nothing to do with Brody's purse or anything like that because all that was sorted, right?

Mr Idle made us wait until afternoon to announce who had won the trip to Radio Fantastico. Talk about stretching things out. Don't even try to imagine how I was feeling because you couldn't.

Naz had already worked out the winners. Us. 'I'm going to get Tara Kitson to sign my arm,' he bragged as we waited for registration. Peeling back his sleeve, he showed us a rectangle of dotted lines in felt-tip. 'I've marked the spot for her.'

Dwight goes: 'You should have drawn one on your bum—she'd have had more space!'

Aimee and me laughed at the same time. Do you know, even though she hadn't collected a penny, even though her dad thought it was all a big rip-off, it turned out she was just as excited as Dwight and Naz about the trip to the radio station now that she thought we had genuinely won. 'Dad bought me one of those disposable cameras to take and I've got to ask for a signed photo—one for the whole family,' she said, her eyes shining.

'Do they do those?' I asked. My voice came out low and breathless because I had butterflies in my stomach I was trying to blank out.

Aimee nodded hard. 'Yeah, they do—they're in the foyer as you go in—Dad's seen 'em when he goes to mend the coffee machines.'

'Oh.'

Aimee pushed back my hair and whispered in my ear, 'You can come round to ours for tea tomorrow, if you like. Dad says it's OK, he'll drop you off at your dad's when you're ready.'

'Oh. Thanks,' I said, trying to hide my shock.

She gave me the most enormous smile. 'No worries, Sam. They like me having my best friend round.'

Best friend. That's what she actually called me. You'll hate me for saying it, but that made me really happy. I was in her good books again. Everything was turning out perfect.

Mr Idle walked in then and the whole class stopped talking. Smile, keep calm, I kept saying in my head. Smile, keep calm, no one knows about Brody's money, everything's going perfectly.

'Good afternoon, everyone,' Mr Idle goes, a big smirk on his face. 'In a minute I'm going to announce which table is going to the radio station . . .'

There was a shuffling of bottoms on seats. Naz leaned back on his chair and examined his fingernails, Aimee elbowed me and then linked her arm through mine. It made it hard to concentrate on what Mr Idle was saying when she did that. The butterflies in my stomach had to change direction and crashed into

each other. 'Stop it,' I told them. 'Smile instead. Keep calm, like me.'

Mr Idle carried on explaining. 'I can't give away the total the school has raised because Mr Sharkey is going to announce that in assembly tomorrow. However, I can tell you we have broken last year's total.'

We clapped at that.

'As far as our class goes, I have been staggered by your response. You've been brilliant. Between you, you have raised three hundred and forty-six pounds, on top of which I have added the one hundred and fourteen pounds I made at the rugby club, bringing the Year Five total to . . .'

He put his hand behind his ear and everyone chanted 'Four hundred and sixty pounds,' except Naz, who was still counting.

'That's right! I bet there's not another Year Five in the land that has managed that. Well done. I am so proud of you all. But now for the winning table I'm taking with me to the station on Friday . . . if they can come up at the end so they can take letters of permission home.'

Aimee squeezed my arm really tight.

'In third place,' Mr Idle said, a smile as wide as a banana, 'were the Reds!'

Everyone cheered and I turned round to look at Sam, who put his thumbs up at me.

'What's Riley-Piley looking at us for? Big nerd,' Aimee muttered as she followed my movements.

My smile disappeared in a flash.

'In second place and so close, the Greens . . .'

The butterflies were throwing themselves against the walls of my stomach now. There were hundreds of them—thousands—pushing and pushing and pushing and bouncing and bouncing and bouncing. Aimee squeezed my arm harder. 'Us next,' she whispered, 'we'll bagsie the back seat of the minibus before Naz and Dwight get it, yeah, and I'll tell Tara Kitson all about how I helped you raise the most, right? Oh, and wear your black headband with your name on it and I'll wear mine—we'll look like twins . . .'

A chill ran through me, making the hairs on my arms stand to attention. Pictures of Aimee bossing me about through the years flicked through my mind, like one of those home videos on fast forward. The Pokemon card episode and so, so many others. Then I saw us together at The Magna, her making me smoke behind the sheds or whatever, then dobbing me in when we were caught. I saw her making fun of my clothes and my boyfriends, telling me either they weren't good enough for me or I wasn't good enough for them. I saw her laughing at my kids, telling me they were millstones. The worst thing was, as we got older, I looked more and more like my mum and she looked more and more like Bridget, from a birthmark in the shape of the Isle of Wight to her pointy, Italian boots.

'And, of course, the table going to Radio Fantastico is . . .' Mr Idle grinned and winked at me.

'No!' I screamed. 'No!'

Chapter Sixteen

I am not going to go into tons of detail about what happened after I had confessed about the money not being mine. I don't really want to re-live it, if you must know. Mainly it consisted of Mr Idle going 'Why, Sam?' and me going 'I don't know', and then Mr Idle sending me to see Mr Sharkey in his office and Mr Sharkey going, 'But why, Sam?' and me going, 'I don't know.'

I think Mr Sharkey suspected there was a bit more to the story than I was telling. He kept prodding. 'Has Aimee Anston got anything to do with this? You can be honest with me,' he goes, 'I do know what she can be like.'

I looked at him. I could have said yes. I could have

said she made me do it, with her horrible comments about trailer trash and stuff but I didn't. It was me who had told the first fib and the second one and the third, so it was me who should take the consequences. 'No,' I said to Mr Sharkey, 'it was my own stupid fault.'

'Oh, Sam,' he said, totally disappointed in me. It is not a very nice feeling, knowing your headmaster thinks you have let the whole school down, but to be honest, I couldn't have felt much worse, so I just looked at my shoes and didn't say nothing.

'I've sent for Brody,' Mr Sharkey continued. 'You can explain your actions to her face-to-face. Then Mrs Fryston will need to be informed when she arrives, of course.'

'OK,' I agreed, staring at his carpet, my hands all sticky and sweaty behind me.

After what seemed like a thousand years, Brody walked in, looking surprised and wondering why she had been dragged out of class. Mr Sharkey raised his eyebrows and nodded so I took a deep breath and began.

'Oh, Sammie, I love you!' she goes when I had finished, and gave me a massive hug! I'm not kidding. Talk about strange reactions.

Mr Sharkey seemed as taken aback as I was. 'Brody, this is hardly a matter for celebration!'

'You wouldn't say that if you'd been in my shoes last night when Jake found out  I'd lost a hundred pounds. That guy is so going to have a heart attack at fifty!'

'Sam still shouldn't have taken your money in the first place,' Mr Sharkey reminded her.

The Year Six calmed down enough to take things a bit more seriously. 'Well,' she said after a lengthy pause, 'I guess as long as the money went to charity . . .' She gave me a kind of half-sympathetic, half-quizzical smile. 'And I can tell just from looking at her that Sammie's really sorry.'

I decided there and then that if ever Brody Miller needed anyone to die for her, I'd be first in line. Mr Sharkey wouldn't though. 'Well, that's very lenient of you, Brody. I don't think I would be so tolerant if it had been my money!' he goes.

The coolest girl in the world just shrugged. 'Well, the way I look at it is this—Sammie didn't have to own up but she did, so that's a good thing. I got my money and my purse back so that's a good thing,' she said stroking the pink material with her thumb, 'so what's the problem?'

Mr Sharkey rubbed his spiky scalp and sighed hard. 'Right, well, you'd better go back to class. I'll let your parents know what has happened, of course.'

'Sure,' she beamed, then turned to me. 'See you at After School club, Sammie,' she said and left.

Mr Sharkey's eyes followed her out of the room, then he shook his head. 'I need a coffee,' he said, 'the bell's going in a couple of minutes—I'll come back and take you across to Mrs Fryston. I can't promise she'll react in the same way as Miss Miller—After School club is not like here—she can pick and choose her clients,' he said darkly.

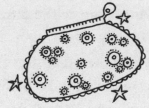

Telling Mr Idle and Mr Sharkey what I had done had been hard. Owning up to Brody Miller had been harder, but walking across the playground towards After School club that afternoon was the hardest. The tarmac on the playground seemed to stretch for miles between the main school building and the mobile but it still didn't take nearly long enough to reach it.

Mrs Fryston looked at me with the same expression of surprise and disappointment as Mr Idle and Mr Sharkey had when she found out what I had done. 'Goodness me!' she gasped, as if it was the worst thing she had ever heard of in her life.

I felt a bit choked up then. I hadn't cried so far. I was trying not to because, as I kept saying to myself, I had no right to cry. My eyes began to get blurry though at Mrs Fryston's reaction and I had to look down at the floor dead quick in case she saw. If she told me I could never come along to After School club again, my heart would break, I just knew it would. I loved it here.

That's why I had screamed in the classroom and owned up. I didn't want to spoil it. I bounced everywhere except here and I knew if I had kept quiet about Brody's purse and gone to Radio Fantastico I would have bounced here, too.

Every time I served Brody cola bottles and cherry lips, I would have bounced. Every time Sam talked to me, I would have bounced. Every time Aimee made some snide comment about Sam or the After School club, I would have bounced. And do you know what? I was sick of bouncing. But I had still messed up anyway, hadn't I? Totally messed up, just like my mum.

Not that I knew how to explain any of this to Mrs Fryston.

'I have told Sam that you have every right to withdraw her attendance here,' Mr Sharkey said to her. The three of us were stood in a semicircle near Mrs Fryston's desk, supposedly out of earshot of the others but I could still feel everyone staring at me. Bad news travels fast round our school. I chewed hard on my bottom lip and waited.

'Withdraw her attendance? Well, that's a bit drastic,' Mrs Fryston replied immediately, 'especially in view of Sammie owning up.' She bent down so that we were eye to eye and cupped my chin gently in her hand, making me look directly at her. I could feel a tear roll down my cheek but I daren't brush it away. Luckily, Mrs Fryston had a tissue handy. 'What it does mean is that you'll have to earn your trust back again, Sammie,' she said, dabbing at my face. 'I imagine Sam might not want you helping in the tuck shop for a while, for instance.'

I managed to nod that I understood and she stood up again. I didn't know what to feel. Relieved that I wasn't banned but sad that she didn't trust me to work with Sam. Slowly, I lifted my head to glance over at the sweet stall. If Sam couldn't forgive me, there'd be no point coming to After School club anyway. Sam was the one who had made me feel so welcome right from day one. It wouldn't be the same without him on my side.

Guess what, though? When I looked up, Sam was already at my side, glaring at the supervisor. 'Of course I want her in the tuck shop, Mrs Fryston! Everyone's entitled to one mistake. I told Mr Idle all along making a competition out of who raised the most money was a mistake. I did, didn't I, Sammie?'

I nodded.

Sam began explaining to Mrs Fryston. 'I suggested a poem. Poetry doesn't make people do desperate things . . . unless it's a really bad poem read by a really bad actor, I suppose, or a very sad poem written to a star-crossed lover . . .' He paused and I could tell a million examples of sad poems were now running through his head but Sam pulled himself together long enough to get back to the subject. '. . . but anyway, Sammie's not a proper thief—she gave Brody's money straight to charity and I know she's honest because she hasn't eaten a single thing she hasn't paid for since she's been a helper. Most of them fill their pockets the second they start. Even people who should know better pinch the sweets, don't they, Mr Sharkey?' Sam added, eyebrows raised directly at him. Mr Sharkey was always helping himself to jelly worms, according to Sam.

Mr Sharkey coughed then scratched at a mark on his tie.

'Well, I'm sure that's true but it's not quite the same thing . . .' Mrs Fryston began.

Sam took a tight hold of my hand. I went beetroot straightaway, especially when someone on the craft table giggled, but Sam was too cool to let that distract him. 'Yes, it is; believe me—I am an excellent judge of character. Now, if you'll excuse us, we have a shop to run.' Without waiting for an answer, he dragged me across to the sweet stall and pointed to a box of sweet-and-sour balls. 'Fresh in today,' he told me, '2p each. Watch them—they're exceedingly sticky.'

'I don't like them,' Brandon said, wrinkling his nose. He had been waiting patiently at the stall all the time, ignoring all the fuss. He held out his hand, showing me one of the sweet-and-sour balls almost glued to his palm.

'What's wrong with them, Brandon?' I asked him.

'They're not green enough,' he said instantly, 'and they smash into bits if you drop 'em. I think they should bounce. They're balls, but they're not bouncy.'

I looked at him and grinned. 'Hey, look at me!' I went, patting my sides up and down. 'I'm not bouncy, either! Isn't that great?'

'Is it?' he frowned.

'It is, Brandon, believe me,' I said.

Epilogue

Well, that's my story. I didn't make the best start to After School club, did I? For a few weeks after the purse business I was pretty quiet, for me. I stuck with poor Sam on the sweet stall every night. He must have thought I was a blob of Blu-Tack or something. I wouldn't even go to the toilet in case anything went missing from the cloakrooms and I got blamed. Just before Christmas, though, Sam got that horrible flu that was going round and he was off for two weeks. We sent him cards and everything.

Guess what happened? Mrs Fryston put *me* in charge of the tuck shop. I thought she would have asked Brody or Reggie or even Alex but she didn't—she asked me.

On the first night she gave me the margarine tub float without a word and at the end she just took the margarine tub without a word. 'Aren't you going to check it, Mrs Fryston?' I asked her when everybody had gone and I was last (yeah, I know—it didn't take Mum long to get back to her old habits).

'No,' Mrs Fryston said, shaking her head slightly so her silver earrings jangled, 'I trust you, Sammie.'

That was so nice of her, wasn't it? After that, I really did feel like one of the mob in the mobile and started mixing properly and getting to know the other kids. Sam's still my number one friend at After School club, though, but I don't love him or nothing, so don't start teasing me about it like Gemma and Sasha do. If it's mushy stuff you're after, you need to read about Brody Miller next. Don't get the wrong idea; her story's not all mushy—even child models with dazzling smiles have their problems—but there is a bit of mush, so don't say I didn't warn you.

Luv Sammie

Do You Know a Sammie?

Have you got a friend who reminds you of Sammie? Perhaps someone in your class has told a big fat lie and got you into trouble? Or maybe you've made something up to cover up a problem? Or do you have an interesting story about trying to raise sponsor money?

If you have a story, send it to us at the After School Club website. We'll print the best stories and find out who is the biggest Sammie of all!

www.oup.com/uk/children/afterschoolclub

After School Club

starring Brody . . .

My family's so screwed-up!

You'd think my life was hectic enough, what with my modelling, school work, private tuition and After School Club—but now I've got my niece to stay. I'm trying to be nice to her but it turns out she has some major issues with me—I mean, big time.

I thought taking her to After School Club would help, but it just ain't happening . . .

ISBN 0 19 275248 0

starring Alex . . .

ISBN 0 19 275249 9

After School Club

starring Jolene . . .

Helena Pielichaty

After School Club

starring Jolene...

... as the runaway who's trying to do a good turn (just make sure she doesn't turn on you)

ISBN 0 19 275250 2